# BEFANA

# BEFANA

A CHRISTMAS STORY

Anne Rockwell

*Atheneum 1974 New York*

*for Hannah,*
*Elizabeth & Oliver*


Library of Congress catalog card number 74-75570
ISBN 0-689-30417-X
Published simultaneously in Canada by
McClelland & Stewart, Ltd.
Manufactured in the United States of America
Printed by Pearl-Pressman-Liberty Printers
Philadelphia, Pennsylvania
Bound by A. Horowitz & Son/Bookbinders
Clifton, New Jersey
First Edition

# BEFANA

Along the great camel route that stretched from East to West there stood a little house, all alone. And in this little house there lived an old, old woman. Befana was her name. She had no neighbors and no friends, no pets and no family. Many years earlier she had been a smiling mother to a fat-cheeked baby and wife to a good man. But a horrible sickness had come to Befana's little house, taking husband and baby away. And from that day on Befana smiled no more, but locked her doors to everyone who passed by.

She put her baby's toys in a chest. There was a straw doll dressed in a little white wool blanket stitched from Befana's wedding dress, and a ball made of a large seedpod that rattled as it rolled. There was a little bouquet of dried meadow flowers and herbs that for all these years had kept their sweet smell. And every evening, year after year, Befana took the little doll from the chest, rocked it and sang songs to it and told stories to it, just as she had to her baby, many years ago.

Often, camel drivers leading their caravans of spices and silks peered into Befana's window and watched the old woman singing as she fondled the straw doll. But if Befana ever looked up and saw them watching her, she glared and shook her finger at them and waved her straw broom to shoo them away. People whispered that she was a witch, or a bad fairy. No traveler ever stopped at her little house to rest and chat, although the route was lonely and the days and nights were long.

But one evening, as Befana was sweeping the dinner crumbs from her floor, a loud knocking came at her door. She ignored it and went on sweeping, but the knocking would not stop. Befana grumbled, but all the same, she looked out her window to see who it might be.

Three men stood at the door. Each one was wearing a golden crown with more jewels than Befana had ever seen. Each one was wearing robes of such silk and gold thread, pearls and precious stones that the starlight flashing on them made a glow like the sun. And all three of these splendid gentlemen were knocking at Befana's door at once.

Befana poked her head out the window and shouted to them to go away, but they went on knocking, louder and louder. So Befana unlocked her door, opened it and shook her broom at the three splendid gentlemen and shouted:

"Go away! Do not bother me!"

But the three gentlemen began to speak, all three at once and they spoke in a language Befana had never heard before, although she had overheard many strange languages spoken outside her window as the caravans passed by.

The three gentlemen waved their arms and pointed up to a bright star in the sky, a new one Befana had not seen before. They pointed East, they pointed West, they pointed North and South; and over and over they pointed to the new bright star. And over and over, they said one word. The word sounded like "Bethlehem."

Befana guessed that they were trying to ask the way to a place called by that name. And although Befana had heard the names of many strange and faraway places spoken of outside her window, Bethlehem was a name she had never before heard.

"I do not know where Bethlehem is. I have never heard of such a place, and I have lived here many years. Now go away, and let an old woman sleep in peace." she said. And she slammed her door and went back to finish sweeping.

Later that night, Befana heard another loud knocking at her door. Without thinking, for she was growing sleepy, Befana opened the door. A ragged shepherd stood there, smiling at her.

"Good evening." he said. "May I come in? I am on my way to Bethlehem, but the way is long and my feet are tired and my hands are numb and cold. Could I warm myself at your cozy fireplace for a few moments?"

Befana was so surprised to hear the shepherd mention the name of Bethlehem again this night that she invited him in. Besides, the shepherd's pleasant, friendly face reminded her of the good husband who had been gone so many years, for he too had had a cheerful smile. Befana pulled up two little stools before the fire and took out her sewing. She was embroidering a purple border on a little pillowcase of fine linen.

She asked the stranger why he wished to go to this place called Bethlehem. He told her that a Baby King was being born there that very night, and he wished to bring him a gift, for he had heard that this baby, although so small, was a very great King. The shepherd showed Befana a little polished stone he had found in the high mountain meadows and a bag of soft lamb's wool.

"These are all I have to give the Baby King." he said sadly, and looked with admiration at Befana's needlework. "My soft lamb's wool inside your fine pillowcase would make a comfortable pillow for the baby's head. Come with me to Bethlehem, Befana. Come and travel on the long, lonely dark road where the wild beasts walk out at night and the cold wind wails. The two of us could keep each other company along the way."

Befana sniffled a tear. She was thinking of how nice it would be to pat a baby's cool, fat cheek, and plump the pillow under its sleeping head. She thought of how lonely she was in her little house along the camel route and how pleasant it was to have a friend to talk with. But then she thought of the dark night, and shivered, for Befana had always been afraid of the dark, for as long as she could remember.

"I cannot go." said Befana. "The darkness frightens me. And suppose we lost our way?" she said, thinking of the three gentlemen who had knocked earlier at her door.

"I can find the way." said the shepherd. "I have tramped over many strange hills with my flock and I have slept out-of-doors during the darkest nights, when not a single star lit the sky. But since you will not go, I will go alone. I must leave now, for it is late." He picked up his crook, the polished stone, and the bag of soft wool.

Befana opened her kitchen cupboard and gave him three pieces of a special candy she sometimes made for herself . . . honey and almonds were in them, and very good they were. The shepherd thanked her and asked her again to come with him, but Befana shuddered as she looked into the dark night, and shook her head. The shepherd waved good-bye and disappeared over the sandy hills and into the darkness.

No sooner had the shepherd vanished from Befana's sight when the sky was lit up brighter than a summer morning. A million stars suddenly flashed and glittered in the night, and where the clouds scuttered over the moon Befana suddenly saw what looked like the wings of great white birds. And from the sky she could hear singing. Or were the wings clouds, and was it the wind singing? But why was the sky so bright?

"Come back!" called Befana loudly in the direction the shepherd had gone. "I *do* want to come with you to Bethlehem! I will not be afraid." she shouted but no one answered; the sky grew brighter and the sounds of rushing wings and singing drowned out Befana's cry.

Into her little house raced Befana and took a basket that was hanging on the wall. She put the straw doll, the bouquet of dried flowers and sweet-smelling herbs, the embroidered pillowcase, the honey-and-almond candies, and the big seedpod ball that rattled as it rolled into the basket, saying to herself, "I will bring these as gifts for the Baby King! Ahhh, but perhaps His room wants sweeping and His Mother is tired, so I will do it for Her!" and Befana took her straw broom under her arm and raced out the door in the direction the shepherd had gone.

"I must catch up with him! He knows the way." she panted as her creaky old legs carried her as fast as they could. Befana ran so fast, faster and faster, that her feet no longer touched the ground, and soon she raced along, to her great surprise, alongside the clouds. The singing had stopped, the white wings no longer flapped, all the stars had faded; the night was dark and cold and Befana did not know the way to Bethlehem and the shepherd was not there to guide her.

But Befana raced on. And she is still racing through the night, carrying her basket of gifts. She stops at every home in every city, town and village, just in case that place is called Bethlehem. And for every sleeping baby and child she leaves a gift, just in case that child is the one she is searching for. And then, softly, gently, quiet as can be, she sweeps the floor with her old straw broom before she leaves, so it is neat and tidy next morning when the children play with their new toys. Her basket is never empty for as soon as she gives a gift, a new one takes its place.

And because she sometimes sits on her broomstick to rest after she has run so far alongside the moon and clouds, there are those who still say she is a witch, or a bad fairy. But they are wrong. She is old Befana, who has lost her way.

3 1172 00796 1931
D.C. PUBLIC LIBRARY